This book belongs to:

....

....

Quarto is the authority on a wide range of topics.

Quarto educates, entertains and enriches the lives of our readers—enthusiasts and lovers of hands-on living.
www.quartoknows.com

Editor: Tasha Percy
Designer: Rosie Levine
Editorial Director: Victoria Garrard
Art Director: Laura Roberts-Jensen

First published in the UK in 2015 by QED Publishing
Part of The Quarto Group, The Old Brewery,
6 Blundell Street, London, N7 9BH

A catalogue record for this book is available from the British Library.

ISBN 978 1 78171 662 5

Manufactured in Guangdong, China TT092017

9 8 7 6 5 4 3

The lion who lost his ROAR,
but learnt to draw

Paula Knight and
Daniel Howarth

QED

"RRRRRROAR!"

Lionel loved to roar.

He had a **deafening** voice.

It startled butterflies and birds and scattered herds of animals.

"Please can you **try** to be a little quieter, Lionel?" asked Papa. "You've disturbed the birds, flustered the butterflies and the zebras are hiding again!"

"RRRRROAR!"

"You're giving me a headache!" said Mama.
"Why don't you sit quietly and draw?"

"Drawing is **boring**! I like

RRRROARING!"

So Lionel did just that – all day long.
Lionel's roar drowned out the
whoosh of the waterfall.

He **shocked** a flock of flamingos.

He **alarmed** the aardvarks.

He **panicked** the parrots.

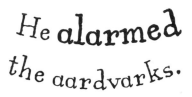

Next morning, Lionel tiptoed
to Mama and Papa's bed.

He opened his mouth...

But nothing happened!

His ROAR was no more.

"Oh dear!" Mama said.

"All that roaring has made your throat sore!"

Lionel was thirsty. He pointed to his mouth.
"I don't know what you mean," said Papa.

Lionel went to the lake for a drink.

The flock of flamingos **squawked** at him, but Lionel couldn't speak.

The parrots on their
perches said "Crawk"
but Lionel couldn't reply.

The monkeys chattered,
but Lionel was silent.

The elephants trumpeted,
but Lionel could only sigh.

"Look Lionel,"
said Monkey,
"you've drawn a pattern!"

"It's a curly swirl – just like my tail!"

"Drawn?" thought Lionel.
"But drawing's **boring!**"

"Pretty pattern, pretty pattern!" squawked the parrots.

Lionel had to agree that the pattern did look rather good.

"Can you draw me?" asked Flamingo.

"And me?" added Monkey.

Lionel could only nod.

He bounded home, and the other animals followed him.

He chose a pink crayon, and started to scribble.

When Lionel handed
over his drawing,
Flamingo was **so** happy.

"Thank you, Lionel.
It looks just like me!"

Drawing was **fun!**

The different coloured crayons matched the things around him:

Bright blue

Pretty pink

Glossy green

Yummy yellow

"How lovely," said Mama.
"You do like drawing, after all!"

"N...n...o," Lionel croaked.

His voice was coming back.

" I...like...

Drrrrrroaaaarring!"

Next steps

Show the children the cover again. By looking at the cover, could they have guessed what Lionel would do in the story?

In the story, Lionel is reluctant to try something new. Can the children think of anything new that they would like to try? Why do they think he doesn't like drawing at first?

The jungle animals are sick of Lionel's noisy roaring in the story. Discuss with the children when it is not a good idea to make lots of noise, and when it's acceptable to be noisy. Do the children think that Lionel will be less noisy now that he can draw?

Let the children draw their favourite animals, and ask them what colours they have chosen. Ideally, make a range of materials available for them to use.

Lionel used his tail to draw with at first. Discuss how other animals might use different parts of their bodies to draw with. For example, an elephant might use its trunk.

Do the children think drawing is fun? Tell them that anyone of any age can draw, and ask them what is their favourite thing to draw. Why do they enjoy drawing?